For Shirlee, with love —M.C.

For Isael, Giovanni, and Diana —W.T.

Text copyright © 2017 by Margery Cuyler
Cover art and interior illustrations copyright © 2017 by Will Terry

All rights reserved. Published in the United States by Dragonfly Books, an imprint of Random House Children's Books,
a division of Penguin Random House LLC, New York. Originally published in hardcover in the United States by
Crown Books for Young Readers, New York, in 2017.

Dragonfly Books and colophon are registered trademarks of Penguin Random House LLC.

Visit us on the Web! rhcbooks.com
Educators and librarians, for a variety of teaching tools, visit us at RHTeachersLibrarians.com

The Library of Congress has cataloged the hardcover edition of this work as follows:
Names: Cuyler, Margery, author. | Terry, Will, illustrator.
Title: Bonaparte falls apart / Margery Cuyler ; illustrated by Will Terry.
Description: First Edition. | New York : Crown Books for Young Readers, 2017. | Summary: Bonaparte the skeleton is literally
falling to pieces and needs help from his friends to pull himself together before the first day of school.
Identifiers: LCCN 2017011237 | ISBN 978-1-101-93768-6 (hardback) | ISBN 978-1-101-93769-3 (glb) | ISBN 978-1-101-93771-6 (ebook)
Subjects: | CYAC: Skeleton—Fiction. | Monsters—Fiction. | Self-confidence—Fiction. | Friendship—Fiction. | First day of school—Fiction. |
BISAC: JUVENILE FICTION / Humorous Stories. | JUVENILE FICTION / Social Issues / Friendship. | JUVENILE FICTION / Monsters.
Classification: LCC PZ7.C997 Bo 2017 | DDC [E]—dc23
ISBN 978-1-101-93772-3 (pbk.)

The artist used Procreate app on iPad and Photoshop to create the illustrations for this book.
The text of this book is set in 15-point OPTI Clemente Book Regular.
Interior design by Nicole Gastonguay

MANUFACTURED IN CHINA   10 9 8 7 6 5 4 3   First Dragonfly Books Edition 2020
Random House Children's Books supports the First Amendment and celebrates the right to read.

For Milo, Happy birthday!

BONAPARTE
Falls Apart

Clickety-clack!

by Margery Cuyler

illustrated by Will Terry

Best,

Margery Cuyler

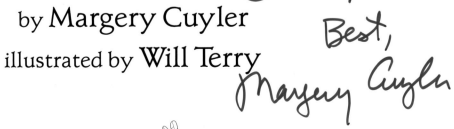

Dragonfly Books ——✺— New York

10/9/21

Bonaparte was falling to pieces, and this really shook him up...

especially when he rode his bike.

Or played catch.

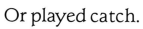

Or visited the doctor's office.

Sometimes his bones rolled away,
and it took him forever to find them.

"What will happen when school starts?" Bonaparte
asked his friends as his hand clacked to the sidewalk.
"I'm falling apart! Everyone will make fun of me."

"I have an idea," said Franky Stein, clicking Bonaparte's hand into place. "Let's glue and screw your bones together."

So Franky Stein
glued and screwed ...

and screwed and glued ...

but when he was finished . . .

Bonaparte couldn't move.

"I can't walk!" he said.

Franky Stein had to undo all his hard work.

"I have another idea," said Blacky Widow. "I'll spin and pin a web around you."

So Blacky Widow spinned and pinned and pinned and spinned ...

but when she was finished . . .

Bonaparte was all tangled up.
"I'm a mess!" he said.

Blacky Widow had to undo all her hard work.

"I have the best idea of all," said Mummicula.
"I'll wrap and strap your bones in place."

So Mummicula wrapped and strapped and strapped and wrapped, but when he was finished …

Bonaparte couldn't see.
"Where is everybody?" he asked in a muffled voice.

Mummicula had to undo all his hard work.

Time passed, and Bonaparte was
so worried about school that his
head fell off.

Franky Stein picked it up and set it back in place. "Before school starts, we will bone up on other ideas," he said.

"We will leave no bone unturned," said Blacky Widow.

"No bones about it!" said Mummicula.

But none of the ideas they came up with seemed just right.

Until...

a dog ran by with a bone in his mouth.

"That bone-lover would be perfect for Bonaparte!" said Mummicula.

So they ran after the dog…

and brought him to Bonaparte.

"What a fetching dog!" Bonaparte exclaimed.

"You can teach him to retrieve your bones," said Franky Stein.

"Bone-anza!" said Bonaparte.
"You are my bone-a-fide friends!"

He named the dog Mandible,
and he spent the next two
weeks training him.

When school started,
Bonaparte was still a little
worried about what the
other kids might think.

But ...

Bonaparte was a home-running hit at recess . . .

a jaw-dropping sensation at lunch . . .

and a rib-tickling wonder in science class.

Bonaparte could hang loose without anyone making fun of him, and this made him *very* happy!

Clickety-clack!

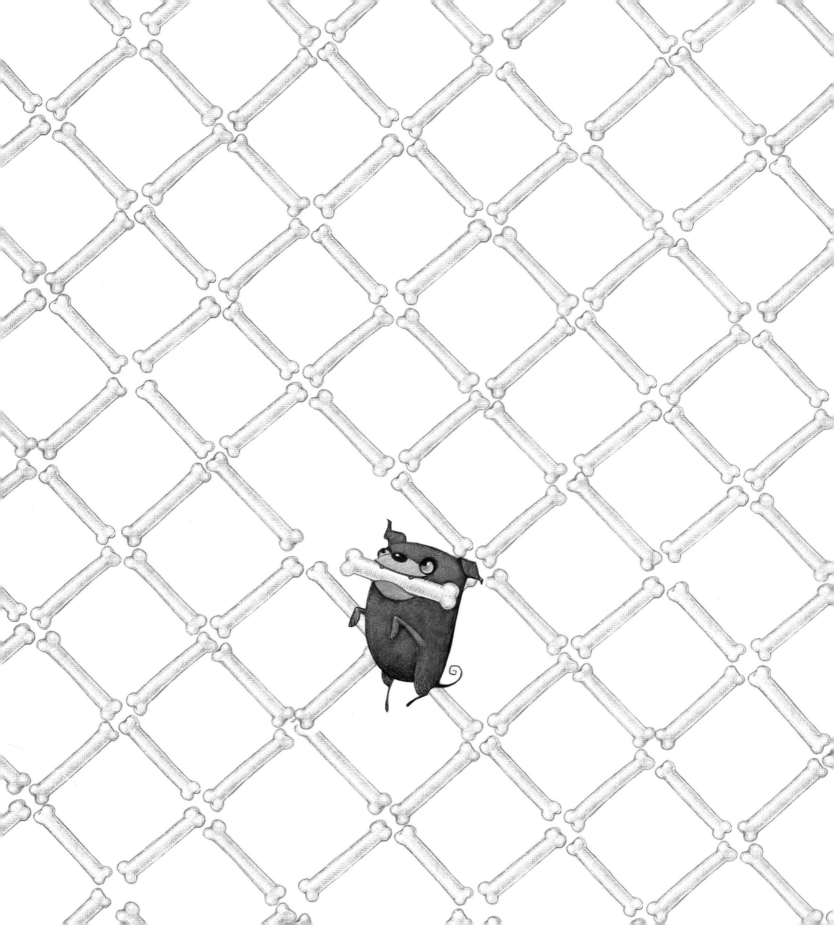